Danny Makes a Mask

written and photographed
by
Mia Coulton

I am going to make a mask.

Here is the head.

5

Here are two eyes.

The two eyes wiggle.

I put the two eyes here.

Here is the nose.

I put the nose here.

Here is the mouth.

I put the mouth here.

Here are two

long antennas.

I put the two

long antennas here.

I go and get Bee.

Look, Bee!

I am a bee, too!